BEAR'S SCHOOL DAY

Written by Stella Blackstone
Illustrated by Debbie Harter

Barefoot Books
step inside a story

This is the school, where bears learn and play.
"Have fun!" wave the grown-ups.
"You'll have a great day!"

The school bell rings and the bears go inside.
They hang up their coats
and their school bags with pride.

The first hour is spent learning music and sums

Then the bears stop for a drink and a bun.

Next, the bears learn
how to write out their names.
They sit with their friends
and play some word games.

It's already lunchtime! The hall is prepared with tables and chairs for all of the bears.

After their meal, the bears have a rest.
They sleep for an hour,
then wake up and stretch.

Hurray! It's playtime. The bears go outside.
They climb up the trees.
They whoosh down the slide.

Next, the bears make a newspaper giraffe.
Isn't she handsome? They all cheer and laugh.

Storytime comes; the bears settle down
and hear about heroes of fame and renown.

The teacher steps out. The little bears follow.
"Goodbye, everybody! See you tomorrow."

This is a map of the school.

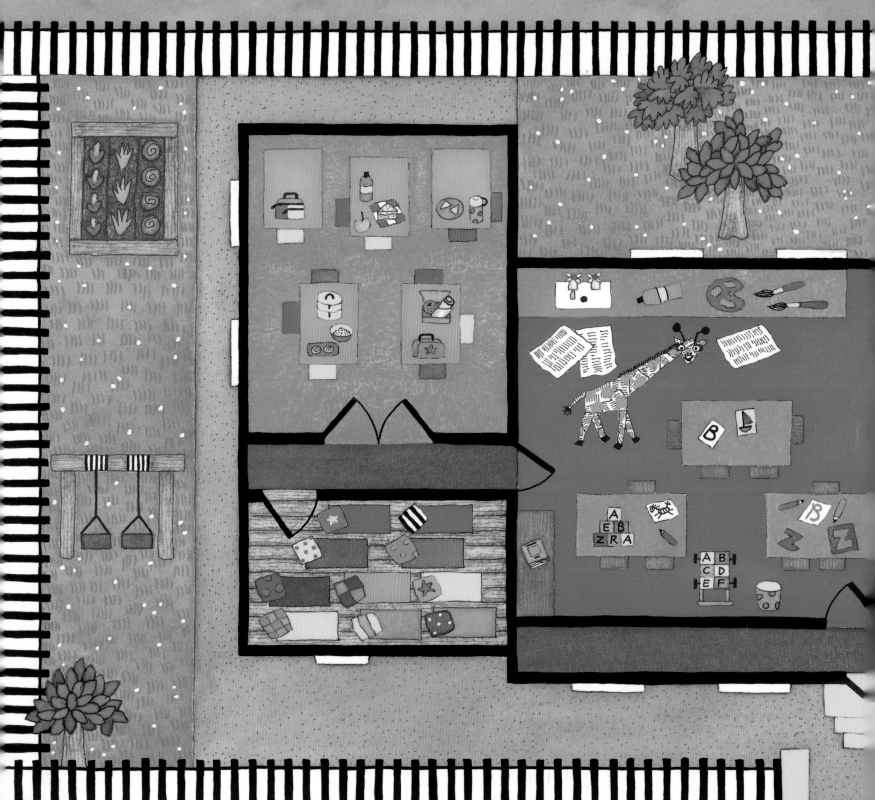

Can you show the new bear around?

For more fun with Bear:

**To the new Barefoot baby bears,
Milo, Lillian and Sasha, with love — S. B.
For Claire, Mike, Will and Ben — D. H.**

Barefoot Books, 294 Banbury Road, Oxford, OX2 7ED
Barefoot Books, 2067 Massachusetts Ave, Cambridge, MA 02140

Text copyright © 2014 by Stella Blackstone
Illustrations copyright © 2014 by Debbie Harter
The moral rights of Stella Blackstone and Debbie Harter have been asserted

Graphic design by Judy Linard, London
Reproduction by B & P International, Hong Kong
Printed in China on 100% acid-free paper

This book was typeset in Slappy and Futura
The illustrations were prepared in paint, pen and ink
and crayons

Paperback ISBN 978-1-78285-085-4

British Cataloguing-in-Publication Data:
a catalogue record for this book is available from the British Library
Library of Congress Cataloging-in-Publication Data is available under
LCCN 2013029742

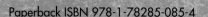